BULLSEYE CHILLERS

Camp Zombie

by Megan Stine and H. William Stine

BULLSEYE CHILLERS™

RANDOM HOUSE ⌂ NEW YORK

To the Brown-Stevens family

A BULLSEYE BOOK PUBLISHED BY RANDOM HOUSE, INC.

Text copyright © 1994 by Megan Stine and H. William Stine.
Cover illustration copyright © 1994 by Dave Henderson.
All rights reserved under International and Pan-American Copyright Conventions. Published in the United States by Random House, Inc., New York, and simultaneously in Canada by Random House of Canada Limited, Toronto.

Library of Congress Cataloging-in-Publication Data:
Stine, Megan. Camp Zombie / by Megan Stine and H. William Stine.
      p.   cm. — (Bullseye chillers)
   SUMMARY: Sixth-grader Corey Campbell and his friends at summer camp try to save themselves from hungry zombies, after failing to convince the camp director that the terrible creatures exist.
   ISBN 0-679-85640-4
   [1. Monsters—Fiction. 2. Camps—Fiction. 3. Horror stories.]
I. Stine, H. William. II. Title. III. Series.
   PZ7.S86035Cam 1994 [Fic]—dc20 93-33748

Manufactured in the United States of America 10 9 8 7 6 5 4 3

Chapter 1

"Corey Campbell?"

I was unpacking my stuff in Cabin 5 when I heard my name called.

"What?" I asked, turning around.

The guy standing in the doorway was holding a clipboard in one hand and a pencil in the other. I couldn't see much of his face because the brim of his Raiders cap was pulled down low. But I saw the whistle around his neck. And from the way the guy acted, I knew he must be a counselor.

"I'm Brian," he said. "Welcome to Camp Harvest Moon."

"Yeah," I said. I didn't even look at him when I said it. I don't like to say too much to people I don't know.

I had only arrived at camp twenty minutes ago. And I didn't want to be here in the first place. I hadn't really loved day camp last summer. But here I was—all the way from Ohio to Camp Harvest Moon in Maine.

It was my mom's idea to send me and my sister away to camp. And it had to be in Maine, too, since my mom had gone to some camp in Maine when she was a kid. Once she got the idea in her head, I couldn't talk her out of it.

"I'd rather have my braces tightened every day the whole summer than go to camp!" I told her. I wasn't kidding, either. But she just laughed. Like it was a big joke.

"Cheer up, Corey," she and my dad said when I got on the airplane. "We're only sending you to Maine. You look like we're sending you off to die."

They didn't know then just how right they were!

My counselor, Brian, stuffed his white T-shirt into his tan shorts. Then he flipped up a sheet of paper on his clipboard.

"Corey, buddy," he said in a phony voice, like he was my best friend in the world. "I just gotta ask you something. Is it true you can't swim? Can't swim a stroke?"

I couldn't believe it. How did he find that out so fast? Then I figured it out. My mom must have told them I couldn't swim. It was true, too.

I looked around the small wooden cabin. Five other guys were crowded in there with me. I didn't even know all their names yet. But now they knew the worst thing about me.

"No. I can't swim," I said. I said it quickly and tried to stare back into Brian's eyes. I wasn't going to tell him that the only water I wasn't afraid of came out of a drinking fountain.

"I mean, I could understand it if a shrimp like Aaron was afraid to swim," Brian said. He pointed at the short kid in the bunk under mine. "But you, Corey—you almost look normal."

"Okay, so I'm short for my age," said Aaron, flipping his straight blond hair out of his eyes.

"You're short for your species!" Brian said with a mean laugh. No one else joined in.

Brian came over and put his arm around my shoulders. "Corey, buddy, let me tell you something. I don't like non-swimmers. They make the cabin look bad. So you're going to be my special project. Before this three-week session is over, you're going to swim all the way across the lake—even if I have to throw you in the water myself!"

When he took his arm off my shoulders, I wanted to check for slime on my shirt.

He started to walk to the door and I let out a sigh. I thought the worst was over. But suddenly he walked over to the shelf where I was putting my stuff.

"Hey—this is a mess," he said, pushing everything I owned onto the floor. "Didn't these guys give you the drill? I want these shelves kept neat—not like a pigsty. Got that?"

I looked at my clothes all over the floor. I was angry, but I kept my answer simple. "Yeah," I said.

"All you guys—the whole cabin—you've got a cleanup inspection in ten minutes," said Brian. "For not telling Corey the rules."

"Oh, man," one of the other kids complained.

"Don't give me any lip," Brian said. He pointed a finger right in the kid's face. Then he headed for the door. "Just my luck," he mumbled loudly on his way out. "I get a cabin full of rejects and jerks."

It was quiet for a minute after he was gone. I don't know what the other guys were thinking. But I was thinking this was going to be the worst three weeks of my whole life.

Then everyone started talking at once.

"You going into the sixth grade?" Aaron asked me.

I looked at him and nodded.

"Me, too," he said. "I know I don't look it, but I am."

"I'm calling my father," complained the tallest kid in the cabin. "He's a lawyer in New York. He'll get rid of Brian before his sunscreen dries. I knew I should have brought my cellular phone."

He started for the door, but Aaron stopped him. "Forget it, Alex," Aaron said. "You know the rules. They won't let you call home."

"They won't?" I said. I felt a lump forming in my throat. I was beginning to panic.

"Don't feel bad, Corey," said the kid in the bunk across from mine. He was wearing his baseball cap backward. His shirt was on backward, too. "Brian told me I was so ugly, I must be adopted. It was the first thing he said to me after my parents left. Well, guess what? I *am* adopted."

In the next few minutes, I learned everyone's name. The adopted kid was Dave, and he wasn't ugly at all. He was perfectly normal looking. He had the bunk above Alex.

Then there were Torris and Nick. Torris had a pudgy baby face, but he was trying to look tough. He had an earring in his left ear. Torris and Nick shared the bunk near the door.

"Haven't you unpacked yet, Corey? What a slowpoke," said a new voice from the doorway.

"Who's that?" asked Aaron.

"It's a girl!" said Alex.

"It's my sister," I said.

"Man, you brought your sister to camp with you?" asked Torris. He looked like I had just barfed on his bare feet or something.

"It's a coed camp," said my sister, Amanda. "What's your problem?"

Amanda is ten, a year younger than I am. She has brown-red hair and green eyes, just like mine. But she's smarter, faster, and a whole lot louder. And of course she's a world-class swimmer. She comes as close to perfect as any kid I've ever seen. She can be a pain sometimes, but the truth is she's a great kid and I like her.

"Tell your sister that girls aren't allowed in the boys' cabins," Alex complained.

"Camp hasn't started," Amanda said. "Parents are still here, so it's just visiting time."

It's not easy to catch Amanda ever making a mistake.

"Your cabin is gross," Amanda said. "Ours is brand-new. I love all the girls in my cabin already. And I have Rosie. She's the best counselor here."

"My counselor's a creep," I said. "I'll be lucky if I make it through the rest of August alive!"

A few hours later, I found out that wasn't a joke!

Chapter 2

It took us two hours and three tries to clean up the cabin well enough to pass Brian's inspection. We almost missed dinner, he kept us working so long.

Not that dinner was so great. It was about what I expected. Meatloaf made with something that Alex called "mystery meat." Canned vegetables. Canned fruit. Milk and cake.

After dinner, Amanda and I took our own tour around the camp. It was about what I expected, too. A bunch of small wooden cabins. Mine was on a hill. A lot of tall pine trees. Two or three big playing fields. And a lake. A deep, dark lake.

I guess every camp has one. Except, somehow, this one looked deeper and darker than any lake I'd ever seen.

"Stop worrying," Amanda said when she saw the look on my face.

Finally the bell rang for evening campfire. Everyone gathered in the middle of camp and sat on logs arranged in a circle around a huge fire. It was pretty neat. First the counselors taught us some songs. One was the camp song—"Shine On Harvest Moon," but with different words. Then Brian told a scary story. After that it was time for bed.

When we were all in our sleeping bags, Brian came into the main room of the cabin.

"How would you like to hear another ghost story?" he said in a spooky voice.

No one answered him, so he snapped off the light. We heard his door slam as he walked into his own small room.

Outside the cabin a million crickets started chirping. I could hear kids singing in one of the other cabins down the hill.

But no one was even breathing loud in ours.

Is this what it's like to be in prison? I wondered. A damp, chilly breeze blew in through the screen. It felt like someone's clammy hand on my face.

"There's something I forgot to tell you guys," Brian suddenly said.

We all jumped. He was three feet away from us and no one had heard him come back into our room.

"What?" asked Aaron from the bunk under me.

Brian took his time. "Did anyone ever tell you that Camp Harvest Moon and Camp Black Bear have been closed for the past twenty years?"

We all knew what Camp Black Bear was. It was the all-boys camp on the other side of the lake. The two camps shared the lake and used each other's woods for hikes and campouts.

"So what?" Torris said.

"So they just opened again this summer," Brian said.

"So what?" Torris said again. "We knew that. Big deal. Why were the camps closed?"

Brian dragged in a metal folding chair from his room and sat on it backward, facing us. He was a long shadow on our floor in the moonlight. "You really want to know?" he asked

It was like a dare, and without thinking everyone jumped to take it. "Yeah, sure," we all said.

"Well," Brian said slowly, "I heard the story from an old geezer who owns the general store in town."

He was using the creepy tone of voice that people always use when they tell ghost stories.

"And he swore every word of it is true," Brian said.

"What's true?" Aaron asked. His voice cracked. He was getting scared already.

"About the drownings," Brian said. "That's why they closed the camps. Because so many people drowned."

Drowned? The word made me feel like I couldn't breathe.

"I'm not upsetting you, am I, Corey?" Brian asked, but I could tell he had a smile on his face.

"The first kid to drown was a junior counselor from the other camp," Brian went on. "He was swimming by himself one day, out in the middle of the lake. By the floating dock. All of a sudden he started screaming holy terror and slapping the water for all he was worth. People rushed out as fast as they could, but by the time they got to him, he was gone."

"You mean the sucker drowned?" asked Torris.

"Maybe," Brian said mysteriously.

I had to sit up. I couldn't breathe. If someone just talks about drowning, I start to feel like there's water all around me, splashing over my head.

"The next summer," Brian said, "it was a chubby kid who went under. A four-eyes with glasses. Just like you, Nick."

Nick was the kid in the bunk by the door. He wasn't fat at all. In fact, he was thin. But he had round wire-rimmed glasses. He was always putting them on to look at things. Then he'd take them off to talk.

"So, this fat four-eyes kid was out on the lake in a rowboat and he decided to jump in for a swim," Brian said. "Big mistake. I always thought fat kids floated better, but he was gone in a minute."

That did it. I didn't want to hear any more. But I knew if I said something, my voice would crack. So I just put my fingers in my ears.

It didn't work. I could still hear.

"Okay, so a couple of guys drowned,"

Alex said calmly. "They probably closed the camps so they wouldn't get taken to court."

"Hey, mister lawyer's boy," said Brian, "it was more than just a couple of people, okay? A year later two more junior counselors drowned. A girl with long brown hair and a guy who loved to sing folk songs. Blub-blub-blub!" Brian was almost laughing. "And you know what happened just a day later? The lifeguard drowned! Can you believe it? The lifeguard!"

"Weird," Aaron said.

"You want to know what's really weird?" asked Brian. "None of the bodies was ever found. Three junior counselors, a fat camper, and a lifeguard—they all drowned in the lake. And disappeared *completely.*"

"Where did the bodies go?" Dave asked. It was the first thing he had said all night.

"You tell me," was all Brian said. Then

he dragged the folding chair back to his room. "Good night," he called in a spooky voice.

No one said anything for the longest time. I was shaking so much I thought I might fall out of the bunk. I scrunched down and zipped my sleeping bag over my head.

But Brian wasn't done with me yet.

"Yeah There sure is something strange about that lake," he called from his little room "People in town still talk about it " I heard him climbing onto his cot. "Oh, I forgot to tell you, Corey. First thing in the morning, we all go swimming in the lake. And when I say *all*, I mean *everyone*! Sleep tight, buddy."

Chapter 3

"Are you going in the water?" Aaron asked me. He looked up at me, flipping his hair out of his eyes.

"No way," I said with a firm shake of my head.

It was nine o'clock the next morning. Just about the whole camp was standing around, waiting to swim in the lake. We were all shivering in our bathing suits because it's cold in Maine—even in summer. But no one had a choice. One by one, we were all going to take a swimming test. It was to find out which swim group we would be in.

"Is it because of all the creepy stuff Brian told us last night?" Aaron asked. "Did you believe him?"

I looked at the lake and took a deep breath. It didn't seem as scary in the early morning light as it had the night before. The lake itself wasn't huge. It was a long, narrow oval, like a big hot dog bun. The distance across was only about two football fields. Camp Black Bear was just across from us on the other side. But the lake was so long that it would take about forty minutes to walk around one end from our camp to theirs.

In the middle of the lake was a floating wooden dock painted white. The camp lifeguard sat on the dock in a tall beach chair. He kept blowing his whistle at some swimmers from Camp Black Bear who were already in the freezing water.

How come they aren't cold? I wondered. Maybe they all came from Canada.

"Well, do you believe him?" Aaron asked me again.

"Huh?" I said. I had been daydreaming.

"About the five people who drowned," Aaron said, "and their bodies disappeared."

"I don't know," I said. Was it true or not? I didn't care. Even if Brian had said there were pots of gold coins in the lake, I still wouldn't go in. "I hate water," I said.

"Yeah, okay, I get it," said Aaron.

The girls from Cabins 1 and 2—the fourth-graders—were splashing around in the shallow part. But Amanda wasn't with them. She was on the other side of a long yellow rope, swimming toward the floating dock with the older kids. They were the ones who wanted to take an advanced swimming class or lifesaving. To be in one of those classes, you had to be able to swim all the way to the dock and back.

I knew my sister would be in that group. She totally loved the water. Like my dad always said: if they asked for a volunteer to see if nearsighted sharks were too blind to bite, Amanda would jump in.

"She's a great swimmer, isn't she?" Aaron asked. "Boy, she's really fast."

"Yeah," I said. I started to walk away, but Aaron grabbed my arm.

"She's almost to the dock already," Aaron said. "Look at her go!"

But I didn't look. I didn't even like to *watch* other people swim. It made me think my turn would be next.

"Hey, wait a minute," said Aaron. There was a complete change in his voice. "Where'd she go? I can't see her."

"What are you talking about?" I asked, turning around.

"She was almost to the dock and then she just disappeared," he said.

I searched the water with my eyes. He was right. Younger kids were shouting and splashing near the shore. Older kids were out in deep water. But Amanda wasn't anywhere.

No, I told myself. It wasn't possible. Nothing could happen to her. She was a champion swimmer. The best.

The next thing I knew, the lifeguard was diving into the water. Like a torpedo he slid below the surface.

He was only under for a few seconds, but it felt a lot longer. Finally he came up again. He was dragging a body with him.

"Amanda!" I shouted and immediately started running toward the edge of the lake. I wanted to jump in the water and swim out there, to see if she was okay. But of course I couldn't. Just standing with my toes in the water was making my heart pound twice as fast.

The lifeguard lifted her onto the dock. And a bunch of people crowded around. I couldn't see. Was she moving?

A minute later the camp director, Mr. McDonald, launched a rowboat from the shore. He was a tall man with glasses and black and gray hair. Amanda's counselor, Rosie, went in the boat, too.

I couldn't see what happened after

that because there were too many people on the dock.

But finally the rowboat started back for land. Amanda was in it—and she was sitting up! She was wrapped in blankets tighter than a mummy. But she was talking a mile a minute, so I knew she was all right.

When they got to shore, Rosie and Mr. McDonald sat Amanda down on a bench. I ran over to her.

"Corey!" she said. Her eyes were wide and wild. She was still shivering and her teeth were chattering.

I pulled her swimming cap off. Her twisty brown-red curls fell down around her face.

"Are you okay? What happened?" I asked.

"Someone tried to pull me under the dock," she said.

Mr. McDonald jumped into the conversation real quick.

"It was probably the boys from Camp Black Bear," he said. "They've been doing that all summer. Fooling around by the dock—playing pranks on Harvest Moon kids. We've warned them a hundred times about it. I'll have another talk with them."

But Amanda shook her head. "It wasn't them, Corey. I know it wasn't. Nobody will believe me."

"You've had quite a shock, young lady," said Mr. McDonald, kneeling by her. "I think you need some rest."

"No," Amanda said. "I'm fine." She stood up to prove it. "I just want to take a walk and talk to Corey."

Of course Amanda got her way. She doesn't lose too many arguments.

We started up the hill toward a path that led to the cabins. Aaron quickly followed us. So did the other guys from my cabin. Maybe they were thinking what I was thinking. Another kid had almost drowned!

28

"What do you mean it wasn't a kid from Camp Black Bear?" I asked my sister.

"It was something else," she said.

"Some*thing* else?" asked Aaron.

"It was like a man," Amanda said. "He was moving, but he didn't look alive."

"You mean like a zombie?" Torris said with a laugh.

"Don't laugh," said Amanda. "I *saw* him under the dock. He was as close to me as you are, Corey. He had horrible dead eyes. His face was white except for some parts that were eaten away. He grabbed my ankles and tried to pull me under the dock with him. The lifeguard scared him away."

I just looked at her. We all did. I didn't know what to say.

"Yeah, right," Torris said. "Like, I really believe there's a zombie in our lake."

"There may be five of them," Aaron

said seriously. "According to Brian."

"What's he talking about?" Amanda asked me.

I didn't want to tell her, not after what had just happened. But I couldn't stop Aaron. He told her the whole story—about the five people who drowned.

"And nobody ever found the bodies," Aaron said.

"This is creepy," Nick said. "I mean we all heard McDonald. He said people have been having trouble at the dock all summer. But what if *none* of it was kids from Camp Black Bear? What if it was all zombies?"

Chapter 4

"Listen, we've all got to make a promise," I said. "From now on, nobody goes anywhere near the lake."

Aaron was about to agree with me. But two seconds later we heard a voice.

"Hey, Corey!" It was Brian, calling me from the lake. "It's time for our cabin to take the swimming test. And guess what? You're first!"

Give me a break, I thought. Brian wasn't even one of the swimming counselors. He was just in charge of sports stuff. Baseball. Soccer. Things like that. Why couldn't he leave me alone about swimming?

"Forget it," I said to my cabinmates.

"No way am I going into that lake. They can't make me."

And they couldn't. Brian was furious. I kept saying no all day long—even after the swim test was over. Even while we were doing archery, horseback riding, and arts and crafts.

I was still saying no at seven o'clock that night when Brian made us all come back to the dining hall after dinner.

He sat on top of a wooden table, eating an ice cream bar.

"Okay, Cabin Five, do you guys know why you're here?"

"We're here because you said we have cleanup," Alex said.

Brian licked a fat drip of ice cream off the back of his hand.

"No. That's what you're going to *do*, lawyer-boy. But that's not *why* you're here," Brian said, looking straight at me.

He picked off a piece of chocolate with his fingers and put it in his mouth.

"You guys are here," he said, "because Corey-buddy had to be different from every other kid in this camp. He wouldn't go in the water today. And till he does, you geeks are cleaning up the dining hall after every single meal."

I looked around at the other guys. Nobody looked like they were in a hurry to thank me for this.

"Maybe *you* can talk some sense into him," Brian said. "*I'm* going to the campfire and have me some camp fun." He dropped his ice cream stick on the floor. Then he left.

After the screen door at the far end of the dining hall slammed shut, the big room was silent.

Finally Alex said, "Thanks. Thanks a lot, *Corey-buddy*."

I didn't answer. But Aaron came to my rescue.

"Would *you* go swimming after what Amanda saw?" he asked Alex.

"Yeah, I *did* go swimming," Alex snapped back. "Everyone did."

"But did you go out to the dock?" I asked.

"I could have," Alex answered. But he sounded unsure. I knew there was a small part of him that was afraid. That believed in the zombie. We all did, sort of. Except for Torris.

"I am not washing floors because of you," Torris said. He sat down on a table and gave me an angry look. "I don't care if your sister says she saw *Elvis* under the dock! I say she saw zip."

"Come on, you guys," said Aaron. "If we don't get to work, Brian will keep us here all night."

"I'll do most of it," I said. "It's my fault."

Nick and I swept the wood floor with a couple of long push brooms. Alex and Aaron scrubbed the rows of wooden tables. Dave emptied the garbage into big black plastic bags. After a while even Torris started to help.

As we worked, we saw the sun go down over the lake through the dining hall windows.

We were too far away from the camp-fire to hear everyone singing. Instead, the whole time we worked we had to listen to Roy, the cook, who was out in the kitchen. He was banging pots and singing some weird song about ghost riders in the sky.

His singing was awful. But as the room grew darker, I was sort of glad that we weren't totally alone.

"What is it with you and swimming?" asked Torris.

"Yeah, why are you so afraid of the water?" Alex asked.

I felt dizzy when I even tried to answer them. What could I say? I wasn't going to tell them that I'd been afraid of water ever since I was born. Or that my dad threw me in our pool when I was six years old. He said it was time for me to get over my fear of the water.

"Sink or swim," he yelled.

I almost drowned.

Suddenly Roy's singing stopped. Then a terrible scream echoed through the dining hall. It sounded like someone was being murdered.

"What was *that*?" asked Aaron.

But we all knew that it had come from the kitchen.

I dropped my broom and ran. We pushed open the swinging door into the kitchen. It hit the wall with a bang.

Hot water was running in the kitchen sink. Steam billowed up. Pots were stacked and drying. The door to the big dishwasher was open.

But where was Roy?

Then we saw him. He was over in the corner, standing with his back and arms pressed against a big thick metal door. It was the door that led into a walk-in refrigerator. We called it the cold room.

"Mother of Pearl!" Roy kept saying. He was a skinny old guy who wore a white sailor's cap and a white apron all the time. "Mother of Pearl!" His face was pale. Sweat dripped through the gray stubble on his face.

"What's wrong, Roy?" said Aaron.

"Stay back! Hoo-boy. Get help!" Roy yelled. "I've got him locked in the cold room!"

"Who?" I said.

Roy shook his head hard. "It looks like a man. But it ain't alive!"

"It's a zombie!" Aaron shouted. "I know it is!"

All of us looked at each other. We didn't know what to do.

Then we heard a loud thump. Then another one. Whatever was in the cold room was trying to get out!

"Mother of Pearl!" Roy said again. "Go get help!"

Aaron took off running first. He dashed through the kitchen screen door into the cool night. I heard one more loud thump on the refrigerator door, and then I tore out of there, too. Roy and the other guys were right behind me.

We raced up the hill to the camp director's cabin. Aaron and I pounded on the door till Mr. McDonald came out.

"There's something in the kitchen!" we yelled.

"Come quick! It's not even human!" someone else yelled.

We were all out of breath and talking at once.

"I can only listen to one person at a time," Mr. McDonald said. He was cool and calm as always.

"It's like the boys say," Roy spoke up in his raspy voice. "There's something in the kitchen. I got him locked up in the cold room, Mr. McDonald. You'd better come see."

"You've got who locked up?" asked the director.

"It's a zombie!" Aaron said.

"I see," said Mr. McDonald. He nodded and a big grin spread across his face. "Roy, how did these pranksters talk you into this? Okay, show me the zombie."

I knew right then that he didn't believe us. But maybe when he heard that thumping in the cold room he'd change his mind!

We all hurried back to the kitchen. Roy was the first one in the door. Everything was just as we had left it—except for one thing. The metal door to the cold room had been torn off its hinges!

"Look!" Aaron shouted.

We all just stared at the opening.

"Mother of Pearl!" Roy said as he walked over to the cold room. "We've been cleaned out. All the meat's gone!"

Chapter 5

"I know who did this," Roy said, staring into the cold room.

"So do I," said Mr. McDonald. Then he turned and gave me and the other guys a friendly thumbs-up sign. "Congratulations, Cabin Five. This is the best joke anyone has ever pulled on me—in thirty years as a camp director!"

"I don't call zombies a joke, Mr. McDonald," said Roy.

Mr. McDonald's face did a complete change. "Now, Roy, you're going too far," he said angrily. "Zombies, Roy?"

I took one look at McDonald's face and decided the smartest thing was to stay out of this. I guess the other guys thought the same. But we kept looking at the cold room's splintered doorframe.

Roy walked over to his big stainless steel sink. It was still filled with sudsy water and unwashed pots.

"I was standing right here," Roy said. "He must have come through that screen door when my back was turned. He came up and grabbed my throat from behind. Boy, he was strong."

I forgot to keep quiet. "Was his face all white and kind of falling off?" I asked.

Roy nodded.

"See, Mr. McDonald?" I said. "There *is* a zombie—just like Amanda said."

"Corey," Mr. McDonald said sternly, "there is no such thing as a zombie."

"Oh, yes there is," Roy said.

McDonald turned and glared at him. But Roy didn't seem to care.

"I would have been a goner if I hadn't beaned him with a skillet," said Roy. He grabbed a skillet out of the water, whirled around, and swung it wildly at the air.

"Whammo! Right on the side of his face. I screamed like I never screamed before. Then I pushed him into the cold room and locked him in."

Nick spoke up. "That's true. We heard him screaming. That's when we came in."

Mr. McDonald turned his head and silenced him with a look.

"The weird thing is, I think I know who it was," Roy said quietly.

"Who?" asked Aaron, but I could tell he didn't really want to know.

"A young fella I knew when I was the cook here twenty years ago," Roy said. "It looked like Mickey Dioreo, the lifeguard."

"The lifeguard who drowned?" Aaron asked. Roy nodded. "And now he's turned into a zombie!"

"That's enough." Mr. McDonald raised his right hand. It was the camp signal for people to get quiet. "Roy," he said sternly, "I'm upset with you. When I bought the camp this year and hired you, you swore to me you didn't drink anymore."

"I don't. I haven't been drunk in five years," said Roy. "I'm telling you what happened."

"I don't think so," said Mr. McDonald. "But if you're saying someone came in here and tried to scare you—and stole the meat—okay. Then I think I know what *really* happened. Those boys at Camp Black Bear were playing a prank. They've been up to tricks all summer."

No way. I knew this was no prank. Roy was telling the truth.

"If it was just kids like us, how'd they tear the door off the hinges?" I asked.

"I intend to find that out," Mr. McDonald said. "I'm going to send your counselor—Brian—over to their camp right now. He'll get to the bottom of this. You boys finish whatever you're doing in the dining hall. Then go to your cabin. Brian will be back before lights out."

I could tell Mr. McDonald thought he

had the situation under control. That's what worried me. Because as far as I knew, there was no way to control a zombie!

After McDonald left, we went back to cleaning up the dining hall. Nobody said very much, but I could tell everyone was worried.

All except for Torris. Every time I looked at him, he shook his head and laughed. He was playing tough—like he didn't believe a word of what Roy or Amanda had said.

It started raining while we were still working. By the time we walked up to our cabin, it was raining pretty hard.

I lay on my bunk and tried to write a letter to my parents. But I had to give up. How could I explain what was really going on at camp?

"I wish we had a lock on the door," said Aaron. He sat down on the edge of his bunk.

"It wouldn't stop that thing from getting in," Nick said.

From the middle of camp, I heard the camp bell ring. Ten o'clock. All the counselors called, "Lights out!"

"Where's Brian?" Aaron asked.

"McDonald sent him over to the other camp," I said. "Remember?"

"Sure, but why isn't he back?" said Aaron.

"Who cares?" Alex said. "Who needs him?"

Just then there were footsteps on our porch. Our cabin door swung open with a bang. Mr. McDonald walked in. He was carrying a long silver flashlight. His black rubber rain poncho was dripping wet. "Lights out, Cabin Five," he said.

"Where's Brian?" Aaron asked. "Why isn't he back yet?"

"I called Camp Black Bear. He didn't get there yet. The storm seems to have delayed him," said Mr. McDonald.

"It only takes ten minutes to row across the lake. Or forty minutes to walk around it," Aaron said. "He's been gone two hours!"

"Don't worry about Brian," said Mr. McDonald. "I'll go looking for him myself. And in the meantime, I'm going to make a deal with you boys. Just for tonight, how would you like to sleep alone for a while?"

"Yeah! All right!" Torris said first, fast, and loudest. But the rest of us drowned him out with a loud "No!"

"Brian will be back soon," said Mr. McDonald, "and I know you'll be fine till then. Good night." He turned out the lights and left.

I tried my best to fall asleep. I wanted to get the night over with fast. But it was hard to sleep with the rain pounding overhead.

Every now and then a streak of lightning lit up the sky. Then it was gone and we were in complete darkness again.

"I can't believe my parents sent me to a camp with zombies," Aaron whined.

"They probably paid double to make sure the camp took you," Torris said with a mean laugh.

"Shut up," I said.

"Go jump in the lake, Corey," Torris snapped back.

"No. Shut up—really. I said that because I think I heard something outside."

"Yeah. I heard something, too," Dave agreed. "Footsteps."

"It's Brian," Alex said. "He's probably back and he's trying to spook us."

"Oh, yeah?" I said. I kept my voice low. "Well, if it's Brian, why does it sound like three people?"

Chapter 6

"Who's out there?" Aaron whispered as softly as he could.

I sat motionless in the dark, listening hard to all the sounds of a Maine rainstorm.

But I listened hardest in between the cracks of thunder. That's when I heard the sounds that scared me the most. Footsteps. A branch snapping right by our cabin. A heavy foot splashing in a puddle.

"You know, you guys give me a big pain," said Torris.

"Shh!" said Aaron.

"I hear them, too," Alex said.

"Me, too," whispered Nick.

"I don't believe you guys," Torris said.

"I couldn't get five bigger wimps if I ordered them by mail!"

He jumped out of his bunk.

"What are you doing?" Dave asked as Torris sailed by.

"I'm putting on my shoes," Torris said. "Then I'm getting my flashlight and going outside."

"Are you crazy?" said Aaron, his voice rising. "There are zombies out there!"

"Stop crying, okay?" Torris said. "It's just some guys from Camp Black Bear. That's all. And I'm going to show them what happens when they try to mess with us."

"You can't go out of the cabin after lights out," said Aaron. "That's the rule." He sounded panicked.

"Someone change his diaper, would you?" Torris said. The next second he was out the door.

I leaped down from my bunk and ran to the nearest window. Rain was blowing in through the screen, making a puddle on the floor. But it was too dark outside to see Torris or anyone else.

The other guys stood at the other windows, on three sides of the cabin. We waited and watched. But the waiting was torture. Where was Torris? Why didn't he come back?

Just then there was a burst of lightning. It was as if someone had flipped a light switch in the sky.

"There he is!" Aaron shouted. "I see him! Torris—and someone else!"

I rushed over to Aaron's window, almost too terrified to look. But it was dark again. I couldn't see a thing. It seemed like forever before another bolt of lightning hit. When it did, for just a second the sky was bright as day.

And then I saw them. Zombies! No, I thought. They can't be real. My heart started pounding so hard I thought I'd faint.

But they *were* real—and there were three of them. Two teenaged boys and a girl in a bathing suit. I could tell they were dead because the skin on their faces was hideous. It was white and puffy and soft. Some pieces of skin looked like they were coming off.

The girl's hair was dirty, wet, and tangled. Her feet were caked with mud. The boys were wearing old camp shorts and shirts—but the clothes were muddy and torn.

The worst part, though, was their eyes. Their *dead* eyes. They stared straight ahead, not looking at anything. They just kept walking toward Torris.

"Help!" Torris moaned as loud as he could. It wasn't a scream really. He was too terrified to scream.

The zombies were moving slowly and stiff-legged with their arms outstretched. But Torris seemed to be frozen. He couldn't move.

"Come on," Dave said. "We've got to help him!"

I ran to the door and everyone followed me into the storm. We ran in the dark, slipping on the soaking ground. The zombies were near a clump of tall pine trees behind our cabin.

"Help me!" Torris moaned again. He still didn't run.

As soon as the monsters saw us coming, two of them moved slowly away. But the biggest one reached out and grabbed Torris's arm. He started pulling Torris toward him, dragging him into the woods.

Dave and Nick just stood there, staring. But I ran up to Torris and grabbed his other arm. I pulled, but the zombie was strong. He wouldn't let go.

And then suddenly, out of the corner of my eye, I saw the girl zombie. She was walking slowly, but coming right for me! She put her hands out and started to reach for my throat. I let go of Torris so I could jump back. But she got a grip on my shirt anyway. She pulled me near.

Up close, she smelled awful—like something rotten. I tried to pry her hand loose, but she was amazingly strong. Her flesh was cold and wet. She looked as if she couldn't decide which part of me to tear apart first. I felt like I was going to die any second.

"Help me, Corey!" Torris yelled.

I peered through the rain. The other zombie had dragged Torris about twenty feet into the woods.

That's what will happen to me if I don't get out of here, I thought. With all my might, I jerked loose from the girl and ran to Torris. The girl kept coming after me, but she was slow. All the zombies were. It seemed they couldn't move fast, no matter what they did.

Quickly I put my arms around Torris's waist. "Help me!" I shouted to the other guys.

Alex, Nick, Dave, and Aaron ran up behind me. They were screaming and yelling as they grabbed me around the waist. Then we all pulled back, like a huge tug-of-war.

Finally we won—the zombie let go of Torris. But as we stumbled backward, all three zombies started walking toward us with their arms outstretched—as if nothing in the world could get in their way.

Then another bolt of lightning flashed. That's when I saw two more of them—a big muscular one and a short fat one wearing round wire-rimmed glasses, just like Nick's. They came out of the woods and joined the other three. It was like an army of dead people, marching straight toward our cabin.

Suddenly a bolt of lightning struck a pine tree ten feet away. There was a deafening crack. Branches and pine cones all around the tree burst into yellow flames.

The instant that happened, all five zombies stopped. They looked at the fire. Then they backed up slowly, away from our cabin. They held their arms in front of their faces, as if they were trying to push the fire away.

We didn't wait to see what happened next. We all ran back to the cabin as fast as we could.

When we were safely inside, we shoved a bunk bed against the door. Then we all just stood there for a while, shivering, too scared to move. Finally I turned on all of the lights and we got out of our wet clothes.

Torris sat scrunched down tight in a corner. He was pretty scratched up and bruised, but he didn't seem to know it. For a while, he didn't seem to know we were even in the cabin.

At last, when the rest of us were all huddled around him wrapped in blankets, Torris looked up.

"The meat," he said. His hands started opening and closing.

"What meat?" asked Aaron. "The meat from the cold room?"

Torris finally made eye contact with us. And then he nodded. "Yeah," he said. "I found all the meat in a big pile out there in the woods." His voice was still far away, but he sounded like he was on his way back to us. "They were going at it with their hands and teeth—eating it raw!"

"Gross," Alex said.

I shuddered.

"It was just like Brian said," Torris went on. "A fat kid with glasses, the lifeguard, a girl, and two other guys. The ones who drowned. Now they've turned into zombies! But you know what the worst part was?"

We all shook our heads.

"The minute they saw me, they forgot about the meat," Torris said. "They didn't want it. They were going to eat me!"

Chapter 7

That night, none of us dared to leave the cabin. Not even to tell McDonald what had happened. We all just sat on our bunks in the dark, praying the zombies wouldn't come back.

Then Nick started talking about zombies. He was an expert because he'd seen a lot of movies about them. He told us everything he knew.

The more we heard, the more scared we felt. We would even have been glad to see Brian. But he didn't show up. So we all took turns staying awake, to keep watch.

When the sun came out the next morning, we jumped out of bed and headed right for McDonald's office. All talking at once, we told him what had happened. I could see he wasn't following it, though. All he heard was the last part. About how we wanted to call home.

"You know the rules, boys," said Mr. McDonald, shaking his head. "It's out of the question. No way."

Aaron looked ready to cry.

"Just one call," I said. "Please."

Mr. McDonald looked at me as if I had just said I wanted to set his mother on fire. He knew why we wanted the phone—to call our parents and tell them to come get us out of camp. But I didn't care if he knew or not. I wasn't going to stay there another minute—and for sure not another night.

From behind his desk, Mr. McDonald reached forward. He covered his desk telephone with both hands. He looked like he was protecting it. But he was just keeping it away from us. "We have a rule," he repeated. "Campers may not use the telephone."

"Better ask your attorneys if you have any rules about child abuse. Or lawsuits. Or campers being eaten by zombies," said Alex.

"Zombies again," Mr. McDonald said. He made a *tsk*ing sound and shook his head.

"It's true," said Aaron. "We fought off five of them last night. It was horrible."

At that point, Alex pushed Nick to the front. "Tell him," Alex said. "Tell him about zombies."

Nick took off his wire-rimmed glasses and gave McDonald a serious stare.

"Sometimes it's a change in the cosmos that brings dead bodies back to life," he explained, trying to remember all his facts. "Or sometimes it's because you disturb their graves. Anyway, once they come back to life, they can't speak and they can't think. All they want is to eat flesh."

"And they almost ate *mine* last night," interrupted Torris.

Aaron jumped into the conversation, too. "I think there's something in the lake. Something that *got* them twenty years ago and turned them into zombies. Now they're coming out because the camps are open again."

"Maybe," Nick said. "Or maybe not. With zombies, you never know. But they usually hide during the day and come out at dusk. The only good thing is they're afraid of fire. But since they're already dead, you can forget about trying to kill them."

Mr. McDonald waited for Nick to run out of steam. "I know you boys had a terrible experience last night. Someone tried to play a trick on you. And I don't blame you for being scared," he said quietly. He gave us each a kindhearted, understanding look.

"But facts are facts," he went on.

"There are no zombies. What you saw last night were people in costumes."

"But they were big and strong," Aaron interrupted.

"Of course some of them were big," Mr. McDonald said. "That's because the Black Bear counselors probably dressed up like zombies—along with some of the campers. They came over here to cause trouble and scare you. But I'm going to make sure that nothing like that happens again."

Zombie costumes? A practical joke? In a rainstorm? The problem was, an adult would always believe a story like that instead of the truth. It made me mad.

"What about Brian?" I said. Mr. McDonald's eyes flicked to me but he didn't move his head. I knew he thought all this zombie stuff was my fault and Amanda's. "He didn't come back last night. Did you find him when you went looking for him?"

"No," he said. "I went all the way around the lake to the other camp. He wasn't on the trail or on the lake. All I found was a rowboat, floating near the shore. And the folks at Camp Black Bear say he never showed up. So I'm afraid I know what happened."

"What?" I asked, holding my breath.

"I've met Brian's type before," McDonald said. "The kind who takes a job and then doesn't want to stick it out for the whole summer. Especially when the job gets tough. So I figure he started to row across the lake and then changed his mind. I'm afraid he ran off and quit his job."

I was afraid too. I felt the fear start in my feet and work its way up, like cold, wet concrete that hardens fast. But I wasn't thinking what McDonald was thinking. No way would Brian quit his job—not when he was having so much fun torturing us.

I knew there could only be one reason why he hadn't come back last night. He had rowed across the lake—and the zombies had nailed him!

Chapter 8

No matter what we said, we couldn't win. McDonald wouldn't let us call home. He kept both hands on the telephone the whole time we were in his office. And I knew we'd never be able to get in there when he was gone because he kept the place locked up tight.

Finally we gave up and left.

"Don't worry, boys," McDonald called as we were leaving. "I'll get you a new counselor by tonight...." His voice trailed off. "Somehow."

We all walked back to our cabin and I climbed up to my bed. It was the only place I felt safe. The other guys mostly did the same. When the camp bell rang for the first activity of the day, we just looked at each other and didn't move.

"Do you want a banana?" Aaron asked a while later. He was handing one up to me. I looked down at him from my bunk. Then I looked away.

"You've been sitting on your bunk for"—Aaron checked his watch—"two hours and thirteen minutes and you haven't spoken a word."

"What can I say, Aaron?" I asked him. "I didn't want to come here in the first place. I'm trapped a thousand miles from home. Dead people are coming out of the lake to eat me. And the man in charge won't even let me make *one phone call*!" I couldn't stop myself from yelling the last three words.

Dave and Nick suddenly came into the cabin from the porch.

"Hey, look what we found," Nick said, taking off his glasses.

I leaned up on my elbow and looked.

"Yuk," said Aaron. "It's the bones!"

"Yeah," Dave said. "From the meat."

"I know what happened," Nick said, sounding like the zombie expert again. "I'll bet they broke into the kitchen to eat Roy. But when he locked them up in the cold room, they decided to take the meat instead."

"Hey, someone's coming," said Dave, looking out the window. "I think it's our new counselor."

I hopped off the bunk and went to look through the screen door.

A tall, skinny kid was walking slowly up the path. He had a sleeping bag under his arm and was dragging a beat-up black duffel bag along the ground. His hair was really long and his jeans were torn. There was a heavy-metal rock group's name on his T-shirt and a dagger-shaped earring in his left ear.

"Hey, dudes. How's it going?" he said, peering through the screen door. "I'm lookin' for cabin number..." He had to fish a piece of paper out of his pocket and read it. "Cabin Five," he said.

"This is it," Aaron said.

"Okay! Time to party," he said. He walked into the cabin and dropped his gear. "My name's Hickey," he announced. "I'm your new counselor, dudes!"

Oh, boy, I thought. But I knew this was probably the best McDonald could do on short notice.

I turned around and climbed back onto my bunk.

"So," Hickey said. "This place is cool. Where do I sleep?"

Uh-oh, I thought as I looked up at the sign over the door to Brian's room. It said COUNSELOR'S ROOM.

Nick rolled his eyes and gave me a look. "Anywhere," he told Hickey.

Hickey nodded. He decided to put his sleeping bag right in front of the door. "I like fresh air," he said.

But he couldn't get his sleeping bag

sack open. He struggled with the draw-string for about five minutes. Finally he gave up.

"So where are you from?" Alex asked Hickey.

"Town," Hickey said. "My dad knows old man McDonald. But I'm not sticking around here for long, man. Now that I got my high school diploma, I'm going to go to surfing school in California!"

Nick and I both rolled our eyes again.

"Have you heard about the zombies?" Aaron asked.

Hickey unzipped a section of his back-pack. "I think I brought some of their tapes," he said.

That was it. I wasn't going to trust my life to this guy for a minute more. I was out of there in a flash and halfway down the hill toward the main part of camp be-fore I realized it.

Now I knew what I had to do. I had to walk to town, find a phone, call my parents, and tell them to come get me.

But before I got to the front gate and the road, some noises brought me back to real life. Behind me was the lake. Three swimming classes were going on. Kids were shouting and splashing. Amanda, I thought! I couldn't go without her.

I ran back to the lake and waved her out of the water.

"Come on," I said as soon as she came close. "Get dressed. We're getting out of here."

She looked at me like I was crazy. "What are you talking about?"

"Didn't you hear what happened last night?" I said. "I'm not staying another night at Camp Zombie!"

"All I heard was that some Black Bear kids played a prank," she said.

"Yeah, right," I said. "Just like the 'prank' someone played on you near the dock." I grabbed her by the shoulders. "Listen, Amanda. I saw them myself.

And Torris almost got eaten by them. They're zombies, Amanda. Five of them. They're real."

Amanda just stood there. For once, she didn't know what to say.

I told her the rest—about how they attacked Roy. And stole the meat. And about how Brian went out last night and never came back. The more I talked the paler she looked.

"So we've got to go *now*," I said.

"I can't," she said. "There's a swimming relay race at four o'clock. My cabin really wants to win."

"What planet are you from?" I yelled. "You're going to swim out to the dock again? Why don't you just pour barbecue sauce on yourself and lie down on a plate!"

"We're not swimming out to the dock. Just in the shallow parts," she said. "And my cabinmates are depending on me, Corey. I can't let them down. Besides,

I'm going to win in a walk."

"Forget it. We're leaving camp now," I said.

But Amanda shook her head. "Think about it. If I leave before the race, everyone will be looking for me. They'll find out we're gone. But if we leave after the race, while everyone's at dinner, no one will notice."

It drives me crazy when she gets so logical. It drives me crazy when she's right, too.

"Okay," I said. "Swim your stupid race if you have to. But just do me one favor."

"What?" she asked.

"Don't drown!"

Chapter 9

Amanda won the relay race easily, just like she said she would.

Before the race, I talked to my friends—who all wanted to sneak out of camp with me.

"It'll never work," I told them. "If we all leave at once, we'll be missed."

Finally Aaron came up with the best plan. He wrote down everyone's phone number. And Alex gave me his telephone calling card. I promised to call everyone's parents from town.

When the race was over, everyone jammed into the dining hall for dinner. That's when Amanda and I met at the edge of the woods near the road.

"It's late. It's five-thirty," I told her.

"We'd better hurry. We don't want to be out when it gets dark—zombie dinner-time."

I didn't have any pockets so I gave Amanda Alex's calling card. I also gave her the piece of paper with the phone numbers written on it. Then we started walking through the woods near the road. We didn't want to be out in the open while we were still close to camp.

The woods were dark and fresh-smelling from all the pine trees. Their needles covered the ground. We were pretty cheerful as we walked along. It felt good to be leaving Camp Zombie.

"Hey, great race," I said.

"Thanks," said Amanda. "No competition. Hey—did you hear that?"

I listened. It sounded like there was something moving in the trees.

"Let's get out of here," Amanda said.

I nodded and we both ran out to the road.

We walked a little farther before we heard it again.

"There's something in the bushes," Amanda said quietly.

I stopped and turned toward where she was pointing. In the tall, thick bushes fifteen feet away, branches were stirring, twigs snapping. Something was definitely in there.

Amanda moved closer to me. "What do we do, Corey?"

"Shhhh," I said. The two of us stood perfectly still. Then the bushes started shaking harder and louder. I grabbed Amanda's hand. I wanted to run, but for some reason I couldn't.

I took a deep breath, expecting to catch the rotten smell of zombie flesh.

Suddenly a deer leaped out of the bushes and onto the road. It stopped and looked at us. Then it leaped the rest of the way across the road and disappeared.

We walked faster after that and didn't

stop no matter what we heard.

About forty minutes went by before we reached the town. When we finally made it, the few small stores were closed up tight.

The town was tiny. But it had a gas station with a pay phone. So as far as I was concerned, it was my favorite city in the whole world.

We hurried to the gas station as fast as we could. The phone was on a cinder block wall between the garage and the small gas station store.

Amanda dropped coins in the soda machine while I picked up the phone. I told the operator I wanted to make a collect call. I gave her our home phone number.

The phone rang once. I couldn't wait to talk to my mom. Twice. Where was she? Wasn't it dinnertime? When it had rung sixteen times, I finally hung up. "They're not home," I said.

"I've told them a hundred million times to get an answering machine," Amanda grumped.

"Never mind," I said "Give me Alex's calling card and the other guys' phone numbers. *Someone's* parents have got to be home."

Amanda reached into the pocket of her shorts. But she didn't take her hand out right away. A weird look crept onto her face.

"Uh-oh," she said, pulling out the paper with the phone numbers on it.

The paper was damp. And all the ink was smeared. You couldn't read a single phone number.

"I'm wearing my bathing suit under my shorts," Amanda explained. "I guess the wet soaked through."

"What now?" I wondered out loud.

We stood by the phone and drank Amanda's soda. A car pulled into the gas station. A police car. The officer got out.

Was he looking for us? Had McDonald discovered we were missing and called the cops?

The officer glanced at us but went into the store.

"Pick up the phone and pretend you're talking," I told my sister.

She did what I said. But it didn't help. When the officer came out of the store eating an ice cream sandwich, he walked right over to us.

He was tall and muscular and everything jingled as he walked. His holster, his handcuffs, his walkie-talkie. "Are you kids okay?" he asked.

Okay? We were cold and hungry and scared and our parents weren't home.

Amanda spoke first. "No," she said.

"No," I agreed.

The officer nodded thoughtfully and said, "Let's talk about it. Do you like ice cream?"

A minute or so later, the three of us

were leaning back against his police car, eating ice cream. Amanda and I were telling him the whole story, start to finish.

"It all started when Amanda went swimming in the lake," I began.

The officer, whose name turned out to be Brubaker, was nothing like Mr. Mc-Donald. He listened to everything we said without interrupting or even giving us funny looks. He nodded thoughtfully the whole time. Once in a while he licked ice cream out of his thick mustache.

"So that's why we ran away," I said, finishing the story.

Officer Brubaker gave me a serious nod. "So dead zombies are trying to eat you," he said.

"I know it sounds crazy, but you've got to help us," I said.

"I will," he said. "Don't worry. I'm going to find out what's going on out there. Climb in the car. I'll take you some-place where you'll be safe."

It's a good thing the police car had seat belts in back, because it was a fast ride. Trees, bushes, and road signs went by in a blur. Officer Brubaker slowed down just enough to make a right turn without the wheels leaving the ground.

"Hey! Wait a minute!" I shouted. "This is the camp!"

In no time at all Amanda and I were back in McDonald's office. The camp director stood in front of us and the police officer blocked the door.

"Thanks for bringing them back," Mr. McDonald said to Brubaker

Brubaker smiled. "No problem," he said. Then he shook his head and laughed. "Zombies!" he said. "Boy oh boy! It's amazing what stories kids will make up when they're homesick!"

Chapter 10

I felt angry and tricked. And worst of all, I was right back where I started from—Camp Zombie!

Outside Mr. McDonald's office window, bats were swooping low, hunting for insects. It was almost sunset. Almost time for the zombies to come out.

I wanted to run to my cabin, climb into my bunk, and zip my sleeping bag over my head.

But after Officer Brubaker left, McDonald had more bad news. He reminded me my cabin was scheduled for an overnight. That meant we were all supposed to spend the night sleeping in tents, in the woods.

And guess how we were getting there?

We were going to row across the lake! We had to, because the campsite was on the Camp Black Bear side of the lake. Not exactly near Camp Black Bear—more like diagonally across from our camp. Anyway the lake was too long to hike around with our gear. The only easy way to get there was to row across.

When Amanda heard that, she threw a fit. She knew how much I hated the water—even in a boat. And she didn't want to be separated from me either—not with the zombies on the loose. So she talked McDonald into letting her go on the overnight, too. As I said, she doesn't lose many arguments.

About twenty minutes later, we all met down at the lake. As we loaded up a long canoe and a rowboat, I told my friends about the trip to town. And how I couldn't call their parents because the phone numbers got wet.

Everyone forgave me except Torris.

After seeing the zombies, he wanted out of there even more than I did.

The other guys were even nice about my fear of the water. They told Hickey to let me climb into the canoe before they pushed off from shore. That way I didn't have to put my feet in the water.

Then we started across the lake, one rowboat, one canoe, six guys, one girl, and one useless counselor. I held on tight as the canoe slipped through the water. No one said a word, but the air was alive. Dusk was coming, and strange sounds and smells owned the lake that night. An owl called out, and it sounded like a warning to me. "Turn back."

I didn't know where the zombies were, but I knew we were being watched. And just being out on the lake was making my heart beat faster.

On the other side of the lake, I didn't feel much better. We quickly walked into the edge of the woods to set up camp.

"What do we do now?" asked Hickey.

"Put up tents," said Alex.

Everyone moved fast except Hickey. He pretended he was trying to decide where to put his tent. But I knew the truth. He couldn't figure out *how* to put it up! Finally Amanda helped him.

While the other guys worked on the tents, Nick and I got a fire going. A big bright fire that no zombie could miss.

"Hey, dudes. Want to hear a ghost story?" Hickey asked, sitting by the fire.

Seven voices answered, "No."

"Listen, Hickey," said Torris. "We're *living* a ghost story! There are zombies out there in the woods. And they want to eat your face. We're sitting in their backyard."

Hickey laughed. "Old McDonald told me you guys would try to scare me," he said. "Heh, heh."

"You *should* be scared," said Torris.

I stared into the fire to try to shut out

their voices. Talking about the zombies was only making me feel worse.

"Hey, look at that. Hickey's tent is falling over," said Dave.

I looked over at our counselor's blue tent. It was leaning to one side.

"Good job of pitching a tent," Torris teased Amanda. "But it's not supposed to fall over until he gets in it."

Amanda stared wide-eyed at the tent. "It's not falling," she said. "It's moving!"

I jumped to my feet.

"Something's in there!" yelled Dave.

The sides of the tent bulged out and in. It was shaking on its stakes.

"It's the zombies!" Aaron shouted.

I pulled Amanda around to the other side of the fire. I wanted to be sure the flames were between us and the tent. Everyone stood there with us.

For a minute, the tent just shook. Then it came crashing down. It was draped over a twisting body. There seemed to be only one zombie in the tent. But it was huge! It fought to get out.

With a loud rip, one side of the nylon suddenly tore in half. I reached out and grabbed the cool end of a burning stick. I wanted to have some fire handy.

That's when a furry black head poked through the hole and looked back at us.

"It's not a zombie. It's a bear!" said Amanda.

The light from our campfire made the dark fur on the animal's head gleam and its eyes glow. Its mouth was frothy white.

We all let out a sigh of relief. Until the bear started walking toward us.

"Hey—don't bears eat people too?" Hickey said.

Aaron grabbed a pan off the ground and started banging it with a stick. I shouted at the bear. Maybe it wasn't the smartest thing for either of us to do—but it worked. The bear turned around and bounded off into the woods.

"Guess I'm not sleeping in there tonight," Hickey said. He went over and looked at his shredded tent.

Then he picked up a small white cardboard box. "Oh, no. That bear chomped all my Twinkies!"

"You're kidding. You left *food* in your tent?" Alex said.

"Midnight snack," Hickey said.

"I don't believe it. You're never supposed to leave any food in your tent. That's rule number one," Alex said.

Torris rolled his eyes. "Don't you know anything, man? Bears can smell food a mile away."

"Yeah," Nick said. "You're supposed to put all the food far away from the campsite."

Hickey nodded slowly. "Wow. Like, this is turning out to be a real learning experience," he said.

I huddled by the fire. Forget the tents. Forget the sleeping bag. Forget sleeping!

I wouldn't sleep another minute till I was miles away from Camp Zombie. Tonight I was staying by the fire. And big surprise. Everyone else decided to stay by the fire with me.

The moon came out, but it looked sickly through gauze-bandage clouds.

"Listen," said Amanda. "Hear that?"

I heard footsteps off in the woods, trampling on twigs and leaves. I jumped up. "Hey, guys. The bear's back."

Aaron leaped to his feet and grabbed a couple of pans. He banged them together. I did the same. We all started shouting again. We got ready.

"Hey—I think there's more than one," Amanda said. She grabbed my arm and pointed. There, in the woods, something was moving.

Then all of a sudden the bushes parted and a dark figure stepped out. But as it came into the light of the campfire, I saw that it wasn't the bear. It was a zombie!

Chapter 11

Someone screamed.

It was the sound of pure gut-twisting terror.

I heard it, but my mind was locked on the creeping zombies. All five of them were in front of us, coming closer. No nightmare I'd ever had was as terrifying as this.

Suddenly I realized it was Amanda screaming. She was right next to me, her hands covering her face. Her shoulders shook with fear as she screamed again.

I put my arm around her shoulders and pulled her close.

"Stay near the fire," I yelled over her scream. "They're afraid of fire!"

The five zombies kept walking stiffly

toward us, the lifeguard in front. His swollen eyes didn't seem to see anything. But his hands and fingers kept opening and closing—reaching for us.

"Holy cannoli!" Hickey yelled. "What do we do now, dudes?"

No one could answer him. We all felt too sick with fear to talk. We just stood there watching the zombies as they started to spread out—and circle us!

The fat one moved off to the left. He was still wearing his round wire-rimmed glasses. But now I noticed the lenses were cracked. The lifeguard moved to the right. He was wearing a whistle around his neck. Strings of slimy seaweed clung to the lanyard.

I heard another scream. Then I heard running. I took my eyes off the zombies long enough to see the back of Hickey. He was headed for the lake.

"Come on, you guys," Alex shouted. "Let's get out of here!"

"Wait!" I shouted. I bent down and grabbed another burning stick from the fire. I took aim and threw it at the girl zombie. She was the one who had tried to get me the night before. The fire forced her back.

As fast as they could, the other guys threw burning sticks, too. That stopped the creatures. But I knew it wouldn't stop them for long.

"Come on!" Alex shouted again.

This time everyone ran for the lake, yelling and screaming. But it was dark and I took a wrong turn. Amanda and I got separated from the others. By the time we reached the water, the canoe was gone.

"They didn't wait for us," I yelled angrily. "They were supposed to wait!"

I couldn't see the canoe on the lake, but I could picture those guys paddling like mad. By now they were probably halfway across.

"We have to take the rowboat!"

Amanda yelled. She jumped into the wooden boat. "Get in."

I had to step in the water to climb into the boat. I hated that. It felt like a cold hand grabbing my ankles. But I did it and sat down on the seat, a wide plank of wood that stretched across the middle of the boat.

I was breathing fast and my chest already hurt. It seemed so stupid to be afraid of the water after what I had just seen. But I couldn't help it. I wrapped my hands tightly around one of the long smooth oars. Amanda sat next to me and took the other oar.

We were facing the shore, because you always sit facing backward in a rowboat. We could see the zombies coming. So we started rowing as fast as we could. But the boat was big. The oars dragged heavily through the water. And we had trouble staying together. We weren't going very fast.

I watched as one by one the dead creatures came up to the water's edge and stopped. Good, I thought. I rowed harder and the boat pulled farther away.

But then all at once, the five zombies stepped into the lake. In no time they were up to their knees and still coming. Up to their waists. Their chins. Then they slid under and were gone—but only from sight. I knew they were still out there somewhere.

"Row!" Amanda yelled, barking orders like a drill sergeant.

I rowed until my arms ached, but I was trembling with fear. The water seemed so deep. The lake so enormous. The night so dark.

Then suddenly as we neared the mid-point of the lake, I pulled hard on my oar—and heard a loud crack. I looked down and saw that the oar had broken in half!

"Corey," Amanda said. She was trying

her best to stay calm. "We can't row with only one oar. We may have to swim for it."

"I can't," I said.

"Sure you can," Amanda said. "You had lessons last summer at day camp."

That was true. I *did* have swimming lessons. But not in the water. I had refused to go in the lake, so the swimming teacher taught me everything on land. He made me lie on my stomach on the grass and do the crawl stroke. Somehow I didn't think that was going to be much help now.

"We'll think of something else," I said.

Amanda was going to answer me, but suddenly the boat started to rock all by itself.

I spun around to look behind me. Amanda did, too.

Then we saw it in the feeble moonlight—the heavy black tarp in the bow of the boat. It was moving. Suddenly it flew up and went sailing overboard.

And there, sitting right in the boat with us, was a zombie!

His face was all white and eaten. But I took one look at the Raiders cap pulled down over his dead eyes and I knew. It was Brian!

The lake had gotten him—just like it got the other five. Now he was a zombie, too!

Chapter 12

Brian sat up on his knees in the bow of the boat. His face was pale, drained of life. There was nothing showing on it—no feelings, no thoughts at all. I couldn't tell if he even knew who I was.

Slowly, just like the others, he lunged forward with his arms outstretched. But he wasn't going for Amanda. He was trying to grab *my* throat!

In terror, I lurched away and the boat began to rock. It knocked Brian over— but only for a second. When he got his balance, he started coming at me again.

Splash!

Amanda had scrambled away and jumped in the lake. "Corey!" she cried.

"Swim for it!" She was treading water, waiting for me to jump.

"No," I moaned. I looked at the water and remembered Brian's words on the first day of camp.

"You're going to swim across the lake—even if I have to throw you in the water myself!" he had told me.

I knew he'd meant it when he said it. But I couldn't believe it was happening this way.

Brian started to crawl toward me, dragging his heavy body closer and closer. I heard his fingernails clawing the wood bottom of the boat.

"Jump!" Amanda shouted.

The water looked like a bottomless mouth that would swallow me up. I'd be gone in a second. I imagined the water over my head, felt myself sinking, sinking forever. I searched frantically for the other zombies. Were they in the water, too? Maybe I couldn't see them, but I knew they were out there. How could I jump into *their* lake?

But Brian was only inches away from me. And he was the zombie I wanted to avoid the most.

I jumped to my feet and leaped into the cold, murky water.

The next thing I knew I was sinking, flailing around with my arms. Then somehow I bobbed to the surface. Amanda was right there beside me, urging me on. I started moving my arms the way I'd been taught, and kicking my feet like mad. And for some reason it worked! I started to move through the water. I was swimming!

Amanda and I aimed ourselves for the distant lights of Camp Harvest Moon.

"Where's Brian?" I gasped, spitting water out of my mouth.

"He *was* trying to row the boat with one oar," Amanda told me. "But he just jumped into the lake. Don't look back."

I started swimming twice as hard when I heard that. Of course Amanda had no trouble keeping up. She could have made it to shore and back twice in the time it took me.

Finally my legs and hands scraped the stony bottom of the lake. I had made it across. I practically crawled onto the shore.

The canoe was resting there on the grass. Where were the other guys? I wondered.

I was so tired, I wanted to collapse. But when I turned around and looked at the water I couldn't believe what I saw. Five dripping figures slowly rose straight out of the water, moving toward shore. It was as if they had simply walked across on the bottom of the lake.

I figured Brian wasn't far behind.

As the zombies came out of the water, Amanda and I started to run. We ran for our lives, heading for the nearest building, the dining hall. It was dark inside. I hoped it would have lots of places to hide in.

We yanked open the door and ran down a long row of wooden tables. Panting and dripping wet, we crouched under a table at the far end.

We waited in the dark, praying that they wouldn't find us. Only a small bit of light shone in the window from a pole outside on the path.

Uh-oh, I thought. Our wet footprints on the wooden floor were a trail. They would lead the zombies right to us!

With a loud bang, the dining hall door suddenly flew open. I poked my head out and saw the monsters. One by one, they were coming into the dining hall.

"Into the kitchen!" I whispered. And Amanda and I made a mad dash for it. We pushed open the kitchen's swinging door and slipped into the darkened space.

Suddenly the lights came on and we froze. Hickey and the other guys were

...ding there. Hickey was holding a big kitchen knife. Alex was ready to throw a stool. Torris had the fire extinguisher.

"Corey!" Aaron said. "We thought you were them."

"They're out there," I said, trying to keep my voice down.

Amanda was looking all around the kitchen. "Didn't you say they were afraid of fire?" she asked.

"They are," said Nick.

Amanda pointed to a shelf. It held plastic bottles of cooking oil.

"So let's make torches," she said.

"Right!" I said. "We can tie towels to the ends of broom handles. And then pour the oil on."

"Whoa, dudes," said Hickey. "You guys aren't supposed to be playing with fire. Someone could get hurt."

What a jerk! I didn't even answer him. I started pouring oil on a torch Amanda made. Then I did the same for Torris's torch. My hands got greasy. When I reached over to set the bottle on the counter, it slipped. The bottle fell on the floor, spilling cooking oil all over the place.

Then I tried to light a match—just as the swinging kitchen door went slamming against the wall. The zombies had kicked it open! I was so startled that I dropped the match. Instantly the cooking oil on the floor ignited.

I couldn't believe how fast the flames spread. First the floor caught fire, then the wall and swinging door behind the zombies. The zombies backed into a corner to get away, but the fire followed them there, too.

I grabbed Amanda's hand. There was still a clear path behind us, out of the kitchen through the back screen door. We ran for it, bumping into guys who were trying to get out ahead of us.

Outside in the cold air, we all started

yelling "Fire!" as loud as we could. The fire raced through the old wooden building really fast. In minutes the entire dining hall was swallowed in flames.

A moment later, the whole camp woke up and everyone went crazy. They ran around with buckets of water. But it was too late.

When McDonald got there, he started following us around, asking what had happened. But I didn't answer him. I just kept my eyes on the building. I wanted to be sure the zombies didn't get out. I had to know that Camp Zombie was closed forever.

"You did this! This was your fault!" McDonald said, standing over us. His face had black smudges from the smoky air. "You boys ruined my camp."

"It was an accident," I said. "We were just trying to scare away the zombies."

He glared at me with pure hate in his eyes. But I didn't care. At least now I knew the zombies were dead—and this time they'd stay that way. Forever.

When the fire was finally out, McDonald called all our parents. He woke my dad up and told him to be on the next plane from Ohio.

"I'm keeping these boys—and your daughter—away from the decent children in the camp until you get here," he said. Then he slammed down the phone.

By the time my mom and dad arrived the next day, McDonald was pretty much back to his old calm self. All he said to them was to get their crazy children out of there and that they'd be hearing from his lawyers.

That night I slept in my own bed so soundly that I didn't wake up till the next afternoon. It was great to be home. Of course, my parents didn't totally believe Amanda and me about the zombies. But they believed something had scared us.

And they knew we'd never do anything like burn down a building on purpose.

Then at the end of the summer, two letters came. One was from Alex, who sent his dad's business card. He said to call his dad and he'd make mincemeat out of McDonald in court. He also said to let him know what camp I was going to next summer. It felt good to know I'd made some real friends, even at Camp Zombie.

The other letter was from Police Officer Brubaker. His letter said:

"I'm writing to apologize to you and your sister.

"When the fire department went through the fire scene, they found some badly burned bodies. The doctors examined them and checked their dental records. Finally they proved that the bodies were the same people who had drowned twenty years ago at camp.

"No one can explain it, but I can't

stop thinking that somehow you and your sister were telling me the truth that night.

"I guess the important thing is you got 'em. All five bodies are really dead this time. Thanks."

I was glad to hear it. But I was just as glad to forget everything I knew about Camp Zombie. Still, I wished I had seen McDonald's face when he heard: Five bodies, dead twenty years. He couldn't ignore that proof.

Wait a minute! All of a sudden my hands were shaking, my whole body felt cold. *Five bodies?* But what about Brian? There weren't *five* zombies—there were *six*! My stomach churned as I realized what that meant.

There was still one flesh-eating zombie out there. Wearing a Raiders cap. Waiting for camp to open again. Waiting for kids to come back. Waiting in the lake.

Megan Stine and H. William Stine have written more than sixty books together. Among them are many mystery, adventure, and humor titles for young readers. The Stines have lived all across the country, from San Francisco to New York City. They presently live in Atlanta, Georgia, with their twelve-year-old son, Cody. Every once in a while, when the moon is right, the Stines think about opening a summer camp in Maine—but they haven't quite found the right lake yet.